"*The Spirit Papers* is a haunted book. ‗‗‗‗‗‗ ‗‗ ‗‗‗‗‗‗‗‗ ‗‗‗ ‗‗‗‗‗ ‗ limber and torqued, conjure phantom presences and palpable absences, in which the dreamed-of imagines the dreamer: 'You dream of me writing / your name on paper / adding in pencil a *live*.' Metzger probes enigmas of kinship, often filial, and navigates a restless sense of estrangement, poignantly fixed on 'the halo of what's un-begun.' *The Spirit Papers*, finally, and successfully, builds a world—a world built as much out of what's found, as out of what resists being found."

—James Haug, Juniper Prize for Poetry judge and author of
Legend of the Recent Past

"'A kettle whistles for nobody home. / And the wishes you never / and the others you will' says what's in the heart of Elizabeth Metzger's *The Spirit Papers*. In these intimately naked poems love, and the anticipation of love's inevitable losses, lets us see into the endless facets our imaginations contrive to if not console us, to keep us going. The book gives us the encouragement we get from feeling we are in this together and from what's unbegun we're given some hope, maybe to conjure a kinder us. Precision, quiet daring, a decision to not waste a word, assigns a ceremonial aspect to poems whose lines ask us to take with them the time it takes to let the spirit in."

—Dara Wier, Juniper Prize for Poetry judge and author of
You Good Thing

"Elizabeth Metzger's *The Spirit Papers* is otherworldly, but fiercely in and of this world. These poems are unabashed, culpable, bristling with the will to speak. A rare compression is the night-nurse to an earnest suffering, a quirky self-abnegation, a kind of wild irony. Metzger is not in love with beautiful death, but with a beautiful young man who is dying. The work is as magical and as curious as a Dickinson letter—to a much loved friend—sealed in its envelope enclosed with emissaries: lilacs, foxglove, even a pressed bee. I've rarely come across a first book as unconditional, as exquisite, as captivating as this one is."

—Lucie Brock-Briodo, author of
Stay, Illusion

"The poems in Elizabeth Metzger's *The Spirit Papers* are obsessed with family, lovers, phantoms, soulmates—anyone experience says they're 'life-yoked' to—even as they remain hauntingly uncertain of what life itself *is*, and whether or not it all happens in the mind, and fearful, too, of what it means to find oneself enmeshed in it through others. Luckily the poems' sense of adventure proves greater than their doubt, and their speakers (always versions of the same intrepid girl) trudge into the 'no apparent *why*' of existence armed with an absurdist wit and keen sense of mischief. With her 'blisses in all in the wrong places' and sweet tooth for nihilism—'I'd like to guide the grayest feather / through a loom that produces nothing'—that girl never stops suspecting the world might be, ultimately, no better than 'one humid mediocre day,' and the heaven hidden in it, or after it, a fruitless 'chore,' but 'Eventually / as a new dinosaur,' the persistence of others comes to harness her 'here / between then and then'—in time, in life, in love. Like Brontë's 'No coward soul' or Dickinson's 'Soul at the "White Heat"' by way of Lewis Carroll's Alice, the protagonist at play in *The Spirit Papers* is a figure of cracked fortitude, dread, and of the wildly transformative, sometimes dangerous, tonic of her own imagination. This is a darkly delightful, ever-deepening and hard-won book by a brilliant, visionary new talent."

—Timothy Donnelly, author of
The Cloud Corporation

THE SPIRIT PAPERS

THE SPIRIT PAPERS

. . ..

ELIZABETH METZGER

University of Massachusetts Press
AMHERST AND BOSTON

ISBN 978-1-62534-263-8

Designed by Sally Nichols
Set in Adobe Garamond Pro
Printed and bound by Maple Press, Inc.

Cover design by Sally Nichols
Cover art by John Scott, *Head Cluster (Blue)*, 2015
mixed media on paper, 50 x 38 inches
Courtesy of Nicholas Metivier Gallery, Toronto.

Library of Congress Cataloging-in-Publication Data

Names: Metzger, Elizabeth, 1988– author.
Title: The spirit papers / Elizabeth Metzger.
Description: Amherst : University of Massachusetts Press, 2017. | "Juniper
Prize for Poetry" — Verso title page.
Identifiers: LCCN 2016036162 | ISBN 9781625342638 (pbk. : alk. paper)
Classification: LCC PS3613.E8946 A6 2017 | DDC 811/.6—dc23
LC record available at https://lccn.loc.gov/2016036162

British Library Cataloguing-in-Publication Data
A catalog record for this book is available from the British Library.

For Max Ritvo & Dan Attanasio

CONTENTS

III

IV

V

VI

To go to heaven, we make heaven come to us.

JOHN DONNE

CELLAR BELOW HEAVEN

I can hold a grudge against a bird.

The word "done" in your mouth
becomes my mouth.

I dog-ear my days toward you,

pulling a javelin out of a see-through star.
I watch you and all the occluded ones

file out of the night
and toward me

asking how I know it is a star
given its clarity.

EXPECTING A DEATH

Because it ends
so soon, the world

insists it was made
to be permanent.

It reminds us we
are valued mostly

for our greenness
our submissions

by the many creatures
who spend

their instant like
a lottery in a pasture

guessing badly.
Why would god

make heaven
such a chore and

love an hourglass
that lasts long enough

to be noticed
but times nothing?

All night
of almost every night

I walk through doors
until the house

shrinks down to rooms
then thresholds

then door to door
to door so no one

can walk through them.
There is nothing

in this night I would
rather do than float

on your dying
float out of this life

with you and be
pulled back to house

with the comfort of
running butter knives

through molten glass.

AND BEAUTIFUL TIMES WE HAD

As men
shuck oysters
in the open kitchen
I imagine your body
opening
to be eaten
alive. You will die
in a few months
and my life
with you will
decrease
in proportion
to my life which
from your dead
point of view will be
eternal. We unmake
our faces with
pleasures
that disgust us.
One thing I can't
lose myself is
a tongue. After
the platter of raw
rainbow fish
the oyster
comes
ever-dwelling
in its half shell precisely
chilled. We eat
at the same time.
This
is the food
at the crossing. You
tell me the heart
is its flavor
and you will

digest it for me
once you are ash.
In my mind
we have been
having sex
this whole time to
recreate you
in my mind.

AFTER YOU LEFT ME IN OUTER SPACE

I opened the door and found a miniature zebra
on my doorstep. Each of her stripes
had the sudden afterglow of a lightning bolt.

"Have we met before?" I said
cupping her to my nose,
the nostrils being instinctively better to listen with.

It was then I noticed on the white of her withers
a herd of tinier zebra tearing a lion apart.
He rose at the climax of my eye contact

as if about to roar, but instead said
"Don't worry I like when they eat me
but damn it stop your scrutiny.

It's the glare of your inner doorknob I'm after.
It's the yesterday thumbprint that feeds me."
The zebras were wet with lion lust

turning their necks triangularly toward me
and I felt some thunder conquer my left wrist
where the bigger miniature zebra had started to kick

and thrash away flies and the flies were
just barely legible. The flies of course
were of this world.

ANNIVERSARY ON THIS SIDE OF ETERNITY

There is not more or less time, but

a white balloon floats down
just after it is filled. There is often

my surrender, more stubborn
to the pin. There is often my surrender

that lets me ribbon home.

SIMULTANEOUS INTERPRETER

In the provable world, you conjure a kinder me.
Lying in chaff, you would even keep that.

You speak for what ends. Native
intelligence doesn't exist.

The row of shoes, by which I measured
my closeness to strangers, is gone.

Now time, which cracks in the barn,
is what loneliness will turn into. Body

of a slender period that won't begin with me,
where colorless girls wear long gold sleeves.

Their laughter makes veins in the marble.
Your heart will be shedding an era

beyond the body, falling absurdly
on all the unfinished floors.

FIRST RELAPSE

Don't you love
when the night drains of color
and we can be in the same soot
of not knowing
like most other people
whose waking is patience.
Leaning on my shoulder
you are a bowl
holding one rotating zero of lint.
A compromise
we never considered
inhabits you now, wheeling
its rapture up the steep
out-of-time.
You told me early
we are given humor
to remember the mind
is the body, and the body is
violent. After recognizing
its sediment
gravity, I comb
you until your heart
fuzzes over like cornflowers
we tested for blueness.
Why am I the one complaining
about being drained
when it is your breath
I will be pumping
in no time, with my violet daylight
damn-you-dear glove?
All our errors
have wandered tonight
through a valley
through me, revolting from
the wild, whose creed is color.

IN MY RECKLESSLY BRIGHT BUT AVERAGE FLASHBACK OF YOUR CHILDHOOD

I see the acid bones of a boy unlocked from ice

and the halo of what's un-begun about him.

I feel microscopic humans
sprinting down his face.

If he's my first to go I will thank nobody for everything.

COURTYARD OF THE MOST EMBARRASSING GOD

Had you left
me alive, I would have killed
a rabbit for my pleasure.

Our proportion of skeleton to fur
would make me sure at least
of being animate.

The pelt, dead and bristling,
might guard me from death,
a city wet with the rain of better places.

Rubbing the skin so hard into my skin,
it would have been the gentlest thing.
It would have been a better brain.

My vanishing is a meadow
and I know my kill still moves
more or less disturbed,

every leap blowing the shell
off my deformed blue-lipped bud.

I would work myself into the dirt if I could stay.

INTERIOR WHERE NO ONE NOTICES

They told me to stay away from the sill
but I raised the pane and slipped one sparrow
black and shivering into my mouth. I kept it there all evening,
wetting its wings on my tongue, letting it peck at the vault
of my throat. I could taste the color of lava,
contagious and bitter. An hour when light goes
and the room grows a wall and even wood
becomes restless. It wept in the middle of my mouth.
It sharpened my breath into little teeth
for knowing. It was loveless. And I would not have
trusted anyone. After, I was thirsty all the time.

A NEW BIRTHDAY

Age promised he knew
what I was thinking from his pulpit.
He threatened
to tap the wires within me,
swore he'd turn my hips out,
make me bleed. Gradually
he spread a light brown fur around my body.
By dark I taught myself to raze
the buffer animal.
I cut and tied a second navel, relearned
the pleasure of my thumbs.
Each passing ambulance was an affair
in which a cop offered me milk.
Tell me the stranger's unsafe. Tell me the child
is holy. I wanted to believe you.
I wanted to be kept weak.

PREPOSSESSION

Remember, like me,
the history of
poetry
never had any boys
to play with
as a girl.
On an island
of islands
the goats
creaked
the mountains
into roads
and grew old
and grew men
and the men
sliced the goats
until they
sputtered red
and wiser
into wishes,
queen and bull.
The history of
poetry
was lonely
even with her thumbs
and fire and
a little black fib
planted and
then smashed
into dirt. Little fib,
do sprout,
little fib, do
feed me your
greedy pollen age.
I've climbed
the hill

backwards
through ordinary
fog to admire
in goat blood, my boys.

FOR MY BROTHER, IN BLUEGRASS

Ever since you were placed in the 99th percentile
I've been trying to be exceptional—

    I made you the father of my dolls.

    I made you my in case of emergency.

When we walked down the street I was the stranger.
You were whatever moved you.

Either you were a thoroughbred glistening through clay
or you spoke a language you made up by the minute.

Then you drove away to join the normal.

    O Lawyer, let me compose you.

Let me leave you in the prodigal field,
back between boyhood and the prematurely old.

    You gave me up for the word *lovely.*

Listen, the North is kicking out at the door
for you to be familiar.

THE UNMAKING LIFE

What I don't finish adores me,
shepherds me around my first room,

the toy barnhouse sick with ventriloquism.

Under my adult hands the ladder crushes,
a few secure rungs between floors.

I had thought the walls knew the limits

of peace, what was possible.
What I missed: the thing happening,

the thing not happening.

Now the plastic horses have been tangled
and sent away. I was not sent away.

Still I pretend myself to sleep.

In the midwest above my bed,
the stalls are visible and empty.

It is said that the flammable, once lit,

can be saved forever. I taste now
and again the used end of a match.

What would my senses give to lose track of me,

to keep their secrets to themselves?
The distance between us, which is art,

makes it impossible to leave, or enter.

NEVER BEDTIME

I have a phantom who exists only at noon.

She sighs out all the milk
she foregoes the rest of the hours
in an everlasting blue vein
letting me down.

In her omniscient aloneness
her instincts are quartz and full of time
She does not need me to speak
or love or die.

What some call shy
I see as her unconditional wish to leave
no mark
on the most beautiful hour

to answer to no mother no word.

MY LIVING MOTHER'S MEMORY

You have broken my heirloom necklace

and swept me with it,
all our nervous colorless beads
into the dustpan.

I don't blame you for the broom
beating the throat that fails me.

You know you are about to forget my name.

SLEEP TIGHT

When you pull the white strand

from the lobe of dream

where nobody parts your hair

you parch awake reaching for salt,

the glass too dark for thirst.

A moonflower shutting open,

you are almost orphan.

In the room where they say

only the young roam,

you stamp your hooves to loose a god.

A kettle whistles for nobody home.

And the wishes you never

and the others you will

burn and forget they are burning.

BROTHER AT BREAKDOWN AGE ON HUGE BOAT WITH SISTER

Why the flying fish bother with air baffles me
while you're breathing. I warn them back under, plot

to hold them like practicing new hands.
You miss them. Do you mind?

The tide's rough with a steroid-trembling
to be understood. At sea nobody

can stand to think closely.
Even though I am not your favorite

I count back to zero. Your spirit bends
just enough to never pick itself up.

FOR THE NINTH MISCARRIED SIBLING

You swam in our brother's leftover armor in circles
but couldn't manage to keep popped the eye-

white collar of existing. What is one-dimensional
except the yes we both began

in someone else's mind. By the end
you rebelled so hard against the alive,

lilac-faced without a face, less ordinary.
Ether-long, I softened in the walls

in wait, listening with my mouth against the outer light
when you whispered, not born, in the ear

of my ear *anything you love you will infect*

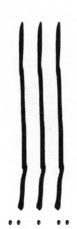

DANIEL

Here's the silver machine, the cold mechanical cow
that turns a stream of milk
into the soft continuous body of the deposition,
winding and unwinding its idle white.

Hold down the lever as long as you
can hold me up.
Let the lever become a hand in your hand.

Let go only when the white peaks and curls.
It is the highest form of holding still,
shape melted to nourishing.

Hear the guts of the machine throbbing.

There is a mouth between our mouths
around the mountain
of cold sifted sugar.

Your mouth when it enters mine
is like a mouth of snow
not biting, sticking its warm
wet tongue against me.

Tonight we feed each other
the frozen tongue,
hailing the cream, holding it
in the throat like a sigh.

We have swallowed too fast
this sweet universe—
chill clinking of bells
against each tastebud.

Gorgeous headache,
sudden attention.

The sun gushes up, a liquid
anonymous light
calling you out of your face.

When you need it to be night,
there will be my pleated blue skirt
rolled six inches above the knee

waiting for you
to blow it gently over
my unbuttoned corners,
a triangle of fact over a triangle of want.

Lose me inside the elastic sadness
where the slackened waistline
still creases a rim around my stomach.

Incorporate your waist
into the widening banner.
Include your torso, your limbs
around my original axis.

There is still a society of firsts
where we will meet,
white carriages loud and circling
the cobbled center of my body.

My body is so clumsy
trying to prove it is a body
trying to hold your body.

SMALL TALK WITH AN IMAGINED SON

I've felt cold enough toward you
to soften a diamond with my teeth.

All right, I'm a little afraid.

It's the zeroing in of All That Could
Possibly Go Wrong vs. Myself.

I've crawled over your first potential steps,
marking and proofing
the sockets of the world for charge.

When the dialogue of one God
is split and distributed among humans,

I'd rather you be dumb
than electric.

I hear you sobbing for me
like a grown-up man
deep in the loins of a white-walled obsession.

See, I'm afraid reciting every lord's and post-
lord's prayer.

FED UP WITH ALL YOUR POWERS
AND INVISIBILITY

You grow only as hot as my hand,
the one the confidante confides in.

All summer I nursed you like a noun,
a diamond composing in the mine.

Overseer, master of what I miss,
a blink can shut the ballroom down.

My Cassandra's about to babble
about a privacy she can't believe in:

bright ringlets of someone else's wisdom
brushed with noise.

When you are stupid and most viable
let me swallow one tiny defiant sun

until the public light explodes a slightly
altered angle of confusion

and you fly into the glass of it, mistaking
clarity for understanding.

LUCID DREAMING WITHIN BIOLOGICAL CLOCK

Optimistic as a disembodied

heartbeat, I kissed

willy-nilly my worst son's wounds.

For all my fertile hours,

I didn't wake unless he slept

inside my ticking—

like white whiskerless rabbits

I let him look me in the brain.

One dream, he handed me

an hourglass of sugar,

then slammed his other hand

on top of mine, when we

were starving for a mouth.

So we had sweetness for a while.

DAN'S DOG ATE A NEEDLE

Dan's dog ate a needle, swallowed it off my second story
adulthood.

Why would he have chosen such a sharp
notorious stillness
to sew himself shut with

if not for a human beautifulness
already discarded in him.

To be unstitched by the surgeon.
To be sewn from the inside back out.

How could a dog correct the symptom of hunger
with a fine art so mechanical
and nervous, the stomach
an emblem of long distance?

It was the pink thread that caused the abscess
not the needle,
the way it caught in the roof
of his mouth and the lip of his liver
and the phantom rim where the soul sits
even in dogs.

I am not afraid of you anymore
that you have suffered the surgeon,
in the midst of your dragonhood, your moanless
resemblance to death.

He must have liked the thread, the surgeon said,
and the needle came along for the ride.

NEAR DISTANCE

Desire is finally
the enemy of need, a city guarded
by quicksilver soldiers and you
sailing your ill-timed head inside me.
You watch me wake to see if I will
shiver. When it's bright we wring
each other out. I deprived you once
of vision, the longbow of adoration,
tightened a green scarf over your eyes
like the imminent world.
Then I touch you, surely and with
the wishful instinct of water.

ANTICIPATORY MISCARRIAGE

I bleed like
a finished funeral
into the fantasy
handkerchief
where pain gazelles
intervene
in the parts
of me
that bleed.
They graze
vacantly with
pantomimed
appetite. Their taboo
horns yank
the blood right
out of me.
They envy
that I do not
leap away. To be
lighter and less
seduced
by gravity, they fetter
sensation
in their anxious
multiplying herd.
I teach them
to bite
better, bite
around my unsensing.
Why be rubbed
when you
can run back
through
the elastic trap
of transformations?

SPELL OF INTERIOR RETREAT

Gold foil babies punch a nightmare
of their lingering cords.

Like shoulder weeds, they grow up
without any effort and bother no one.

Collapsed by sleep,
their human pounds appear—

the thought of tissue, of dimension,
makes them seem ugly in their faces.

Gold foil babies, do you hear
that earworm music
of all the words you don't know?

I take attendance. How can you say "here,"
utter "absent" or follow me onto my lips?

Gold foil babies, the possibility of becoming
is executed in my ear.

AS MISCARRIAGE TO ME

You noticed me

as artifact and then as one who overthrows

itself. I am a little *it* today

don't pity *it* a china cup,

a wooden plank.

I am in the scheme of things not so much worse-

off cracked.

DELETE THE BIRD

My will was just a constant cuckoo
by the hour I arrived, not mine
but calling me the epitome of waste.

He warned me toward him
by an inch of dangling wire
that charged each minute into noise.

I longed for him, not mine. I forced him
with my vision to sing on,
wishing he'd linger like a danger scent

so I'd know he was a danger.
Others would say: "we'll pray"
"we keep you in our thoughts"

as they gnawed turkey legs
in plain view of my ravishing, not mine.
I pulled my eyelids off and coveted

this not mine bird.
Folding my arms behind me, I faked
withholding so he might nibble

lifelines from my palms
bitter as he was to circumvent
my body for my mind, to acknowledge

I was body first.
I let this brief olympics go till morning,
called him Mine teasingly

and made him think I didn't want him gone.
But want in wasted times is not the want of life—
it fights the ground and sucks

at every thought a godly laxative.
Did I want his dungeon-yellow
to devise a new direction for my life?

A death not mine but
close enough to hear it as my own
and far enough to hate its mercy, too.

TINSEL DEMON

Before I had to live in an enormous body in a miniscule world,

I took my round existence   with no ledges to perch on.

Want was a matter of perpetual suspension, a liquid cot

That gave me   dreams of having holes.

Rats were beloved in their brutal habits. I had no trouble

Clearing out the attic of a nerve.   Nothing was gentle

Or faintly gracious. The sound of pocketknives carving

The cochlea.   The wet reminder of an eye.

Then you came, littering space   raising your solar finger

To flush each fold with a pink and orange fever.

When you were cold and out of color   you could not stop

Hanging the world with yourself   in cheap restless strips.

126 BENEVOLENT STREET

In the dark, my elbows will never fit

into my ribs again. I will not hang

a blackout curtain over the kitchen.

Each time sex is made, a vase

exactly opposite me shakes. I blush—

a man with rough hands rubs my inner face.

In the providence of petty shames, sleep is

momentary and monumental. It's easy

to see myself everywhere.

NURSERY RHYME

No, I believed you.

I asked everything because I did not know you.

I knew

tiptoes at the elephant hour.

I knew the heart had cymbals

but could not for a while slam them.

THE MATERNAL INSTINCT

Take these, I said. In an overgrown
ring you all stared, yanking dirty yams
from the ground, those awful orange lumps.

Once they were dismembered and gone,
you removed the arms
from my arms and planted them,
fingers down, in the holes.

You gaped and you sighed, saliva
straining icily toward the ground.

Mama, the last one of you said, *you preferred
me before I was born.* And he pointed
the last arm at me. I did not take
its empty hand.

ESSENTIAL TREMOR

Hell is just the clapper of the bell

that announces you
are no longer the beloved.

The world turns out to be one humid mediocre day.

I take a machete to a tulip.

Where death is something you can fuck up,
the broken heart rolls three blank dice.

The psychic says it says a lot.

Everything blushes but my ego,
now dumbed down for "sleep."

A crowd of phenom-hermits
expects a planet to arrive.

I hear in heaven
the angel has a harelip

and she is willing to watch you shake.

WE MUST OUTLOVE EACH OTHER

In rows of extra-long
twin beds, the invincibly
clean sheets
do the screaming for us.
Night after night we remember

more. It is disgusting—
unable to suckle our kind,
nurses tap their ears
against our mouths, listening for shifts
in the spirit. They crack

ancient thermometers
between our lips, the mercury
said to provoke
the movement of memory.
What doesn't kill us they collect

in sparkling little pans.
They say not to be ashamed.

VIA NEGATIVA

Ex-and-future child, limbo lamb,
you exchange hope for a backward glance
nibbling a mother-shaped flame.

What fleeced you into such reticence
of being?

You visited the earth but not anymore,
bent beside your matted fleecing.

In the book of naked transports

there is no "remember?"
there is no "let's . . ."

The echo resists—
mildly hard of hearing.

You visited the earth but not anymore.
When you did you were natural at bounding.

GROWN DAUGHTER

We sit side by side at a round table
impossibly smoking from one orifice in the wall.

As you can see we are leaning forward
on our chair legs, pressing our faces to the faucet

we practiced kissing when we were young.
Then we are practicing empathy for our future

infants—for me I am her past mouth—
sucking the mammal so strenuously love gives

rise to a sense of hollowness, of outpouring,
of energetic stealth. The pillow has no give,

like silence. We did not practice on that. But
I still rock my body between two pillows placed

the long way to prove I am easy to bear
and too protected to console—

It gets late and mother doesn't remember how
to address me, as doctor or Mrs. or clock.

I cannot tell mother from the numbers on her face.
I cannot tell time without her winding around,

and misreading needs me brave and naked
and dead. When mother asks what time it is now,

I ask her to turn down her death, my dial,
and tuck me in.

AFFECTION IS THE FAILURE OF FAILURE

Sex with angels
was the template for my grief—

I gorged myself on marble guns
with impotent marble triggers.

You better, you better,   yes you

The angels begged me to release them,
batting their sights at shadows.

Angels, you better go home.

*To achieve oneness of mind and wound
one must serve another.*

Okay, I said,
as they called back their ammo.

It's hard to tell if their tongues
were working, or if it was me

who had run out of movable parts.

HONEYMOON RECLUSE

I am hoping for my caution to go genetically wrong.

Find a fold among the unrelenting.
Nest there.

The prudest girl in all the city
is sick with cleanness.

She has my blisses in all the wrong places.

I'd like to guide the greyest feather
through a loom that produces nothing.

Enjoyment? It comes apart in my hand.

THE ROCKING AND THE HORSE

Where did she go, deep
in the living room touched longer
in thought than in life?

There are wheels on my horse
and she must be confused whether to roll
or rock to escape her toyhood.

If you find her, tell her not
to stay in one place to be found
as they tell children who get lost.

A toy is like a thought—
It begs to be ridden to life
but can't beg. I am too big

for her, dependent on her stillness
because it cannot break me
or rest, or mother as my thoughts do.

There is abuse in thinking.
We use it to achieve temporary
sanctity for lives

we wouldn't otherwise commit to.
For all the sunsets I miss in the hall
I crack a past whip, memorizing

a spell of both my selves—
the one I tried to be born from
becoming what I've become.

THE SPIRIT PAPERS

You dream of me writing
your name on paper
adding in pencil a *live.*
You dream a lit match.
When the wish, in flames,
buoys down, its shape
is your mustache grown out
over the course of
an adulthood you miss
morphing again into
the daughter who will never
live outside her frozen tube.
I give you no worlds, give back no
early appetites. Eventually
as a new dinosaur
the wish-ash arrives
long-necked and winged
with tiniest human feet.
If I pity your heels, your spirit
is all one way, so you dream
only of ground. If I tell this
dream to my bed
years away, thinking of death
instead of candied things,
there will be no darkness
left to keep you dreaming as me.

PRETEND

Two gnomes sit in space and admire
how unnoticed they go.

Let me play the third gnome,

plant one flower
devoid of water devoid

of our one true sun, and if
the flower grows yes it grows

then the planet is a burden worth passing
between us.   Quick, quicker

we can make it seem
almost like lightness.

Honey, your somebody is home.

THALASSOPHOBIA

It is almost summer in the hotel
by the sea. The room full of dunes
will be inhabited. Twinflowers
thriving in snow will die here.
Still I came. Once I lived with
the undertaker of an afternoon.
Refusing him, I fed a hell-
colored stray. She was so particular,
tongue to my palm, a promise.
Let me be ruined better, let me
be dreamt by a stranger removing
my hand. I was the wave, was never.
Now I hang my desire, undressed
on the damp terrace, where everyone
who watches watches privately.

STARVING THE MUSTANGS

Never again will I feed the mustangs my mind,

outstretched in the grey moon of morning.

Ours is a ritual of nevers, the lung's nocturne

keeping me awake. In a pang of streetlight

my mother is alive. White elms hurl their forms

against the glass. In the coldest room

she wraps herself in Moroccan silk.

A draft from the other hemisphere calls back.

They haunt my window, whinny for azalea and cowbane.

Down the dim corridor I find loose hairs

and gather the losses in a bedside drawer.

UN-EXTINCTION

Through the dying and the balm and the sham dying and the nearly dead,
a pleasure came in. It was to demolish my psyche
with your body.

We play both sides alone. Too many eyes
and arcless changes. *Your move now—*
that jittery oblong forever jealousy of finishing first.

I take scissors inside me, cut nothing,
only enjoy the pressure of opening
around what could open.

All the mossy creatures you sculpt I discard there—
an after with the authority of ferns.

HALF-WISH TO BELONG

I suffer from homesickness in sleep.

It's still the world, you know,
there's nowhere private.

THE EXQUISITE HOAX

Sir of the sayable as long as it is sayable

you promise to unfurl
a heaven where no one believes us.

"Mine" takes the shape of what is over,
stars more civilized than clear.

Before the fate cascade
I touch up the blindstamped lettering of "Yours."

What light is to the eyeless
we are to the lonesome.

Neither of us can get out of earth's way.

REHEARSAL FOR AN UNDERWORLD

On the back of a spookable horse,
in the first ever rain,
you, my dead mother, arrive with
raspberries all over your white bloodless skirt.

On my back, on the horse,
you make us both lighter.

We are going to try this in hell.

There, seven puppies yap and nip my ankles
and I dismount
to their breathy bodies
and cannot love them—

It's the still-wet fur that makes my
hands evaporate, their tails'
constant comet that lets me remember

your mouth in motion, your once-was skin.
Your eye contact without the eyes

is a bullet, and you are my daughter.

I gave you the secret of keeping death
to yourself.

If I had carried all
seven puppies the day I conceived you,
maybe my grip would distract you
from disappearing.

FIGMENT DAUGHTER

I had forgotten how to be selfish
with darkness so you were born

all night, laboring in.

I hoped the skull, like a planet,
would be gentle,

yes, for your brain to diminish.

How would we both host empires now?
Whenever you root for my invisible tit

all the love in the world
amounts to negative one.

FOR MY BROTHER, BACK HOME

House of my living
father's darkness

fixation, forbidding a minute
of halogen in the hall. My brother,

only his son by the way he fixes
his tie, blind-fingered, looking

through the wall. I am also his.

Our perfectionist skeleton.
The bright room I tuck myself in

where I shut the door I open.

THE ECLIPSE THAT QUENCHED THE EGO

Fold yourself inward, world.

Draw me a map of all the missing
rivers you dried,

a star-thread species
nobody could keep in the grave.

Harness me here
between then and then,

a bother of space,
artifact of dark.

It used to be chaos
was a kind of quiet.

A mountain let itself down.

Make me the woman composed
in her own face.

Gather your thunders in my skirt.

POSTMORTEM FAIRYTALE

Once before time, I was
the awkward damsel
with a wry network of delusions.
I fucked a buff enchantment
until desert sun

revealed him to be a fact
of my own desperation.
Over a breakfast of quartz,
he defined time as the nature of our
never being done.

Dread, my pretty suicidal
roommate, insisted on hanging out
forever. Her blonde hairs
still wave at the back of my chair.
Turns out she was

fucking him too.
When they placed the gas lamp
in my mouth,
my reflex away from heat
caused my jaw to unhinge.

It does not need to be told
that the minute the jaw
became useless to me
was also the first I enjoyed.
To think in language without

the chance to speak is
the closest I've come to understanding.
The impeded impulse,
my limestone moat
complete with platelet-colored water.

It does not need to be known
that my eyes are armed
by turrets to know
I am gone except for
the admission of failures,

the prehistoric odor
of my ambitions dripping
from the stalactite of my brain.
It does not need to be felt that the wasp
on my palette

had any desire to obliterate
my taste for taste.
The urgent turned prosthetic,
neat as a foreign film.
Thank you, wasp,

for surrounding me with noise
I never needed, a reverent blackening
genre of disappearing
into my own broke medium.
Good night. If I lie suddenly

with my shadow incorporated
and an alien idea
gagging my face, let me be
kept above ground in the thoughtless
mausoleum of hands.

Enchantment and dread will advise
moving on, but as long
as my body outlasts me,
I would like to be touched harder
to be pressed down.

CARGO

The sky has the salt impediments
of thought. It wants to know

just what exactly it thinks,
but we know the sky is a fact,

just gas and distance, an observation.
The minutes, precocious, exceed the days here,

measured by the appetite of eels.
The feeling of blood as interior shadow

is enough to hold us back
from our lips, from any intention.

We think of what we once were,
a bypassed island

we carried into our guilt.
Once I loved you simply because

it made me feel truthful, like a ship.
Now I love without integrity.

There is no depth but there is
because the ship is going into it.

PRE-ELEGY

In the first year without laughter
what hasn't ever happened hasn't—yet.

A box opens in the stillness
tranquil as any other wish-you-were-here.

In one minute of too much trouble,
everyone who blows an eyelash discloses

a gun. Nobody learns to drive.
Tired girls take drugs to sleep, are dragged

through collective dreams
where the mind is nowhere to be found.

A past thought is ordered and refused.
Someone, for everyone, won't change.

VOICE BOX IN THE SURGICAL FIELD

An automatic train car returns

around existence with the black-
blow cargo of no apparent *why.*

At home a rat collapses beneath a door.

I knock, circled by the chance
you will expire.

Body that appears only by your
body's disappearance—

soon your rib must rotate, like a turnstile,
to let me in.

THE ELEPHANT IN YOUR ROOM

I want to be massive enough
to withstand all the birds, and lazy
enough to move one part of me repeatedly
and still be seen as a whole
that restores you. Both of us

have a small pool of green
cucumber-scented spa water
we splash up around our separate naked selves
and terrify others with. They say "Oh you are so dramatic"
but *you* are the play now—

You have divided your brain
into several rafters and are swinging together
the middle, beginning, and end.
Your eyelashes flutter those red
mannerist curtains, and I say

"I like knowing how much of a stage this is"
and you tell me the colors don't work
the way I think, by absorbing, but
that our eyes choose first
what they are most ready to pursue.

I am ready to be a color,
so when you are in the ground or in your
million ashes I will kneel down. I will seek
out your ashes and sift them from dirt.
Then when I see the white handlebar

in the hotel shower, I will think of
your first bone
with its soft deformed ambitions,
and I will ask how much you discovered
by loving, and how much you lied.

COSMIC CATCH

Tossing the vast light box
in a sterile arc against our orbit,

half of me hoped you would
toss it back empty.

Half of me hoped it would land at my feet
and be full of you.

FRACTION

I am learning to forget numbers
and trust in numbers.

I am counting
the number of minutes left
on a bright song.

I count down the minutes
until I arrive at your house
and then I count down the minutes until I can leave.

I do not go home. I have no important
duty. I have no hungry dog.

When it is time to leave
you do not hug me as you used to.

You put out your hand to high five.

The song is a pause.

The sound of the world is also
a pause, but a slow infinity.

JOINED AT THE DAEMON

Hidden twin,
you are so well-mustached.
Are you famous already?

With real palms and prosthetic
fingers, your horrible noisemaking claps

fill the crowded lounge
with speechlessness.

Your jukebox soul sings me
a diamond, shredded by sun
into a little more time.

It deposits new wants
onto my tongue, and goes quiet.

We twirl and twirl
through an extra-large gown

sweeping one corner
of chance with the length
of your countdown to life.

THIRD NATURE

Be honest, as water. Then ask

what do you fumble in
your roots for?

We are still death-bound darlings,

life-yoked
before we can split.

LUNATIC DIVESTMENT

When you were dead I vandalized
the walls of the green room
where waiting was revived

as an activity. I kicked the plaster
and you kissed me, like a window
that kept you in the wall

so long. Lend me patience
to break just enough at the joints
to see the limits breathe

along their ecstasy plates.
Pathos, the ointment that
made us flesh instead of nothing.

Wipe my mouth with the rag
of my bad words, or maybe
shut my better eye in service

to the blinder one. Who will take
the mountain out from under
Everest? I will wait the body out.

DREAM IN WHICH YOU SURVIVE

In the dream, you are not dying anymore
and you are livid you were not informed sooner
Who changed their mind?—Here

you had made all the preparations, decided
that death is the necessary abacus of love.

Now you must behead the facts
of the bald unachievable annus mirabilis
of your never yet turning
twenty-five. Apartheid of stars—

You're blue again, semi-generous with
the mixing of elements you don't believe in.

The arch in your foot will go on forever
after the matter of you ends.

NOT SPRING

When all the other trees are bare
the red tree grows.

The fire of a thousand parrots
cannot overcome its courage.

I picture you lying in the township
of your father's arms.

The noose of your mouth
is a way of not speaking.

The floors of your eyes, shiny
and light-soaked.

Rest finds your ribcage.
It hides and seeks within

the crescent lung,
a sad little Mesopotamia.

I will be talking to you
for a long time when you wake

in the felt shade, leaving
what you love of what you love.

ACKNOWLEDGMENTS

Thank you to the editors of the following anthologies and journals in which these poems first appeared, sometimes in slightly different forms: *The Adroit Journal*, *BOMB*, *Boston Review*, *Best New Poets 2015*, *Columbia Journal Catch & Release*, *The Common*, *EK-PHRA-SIS (The Home School)*, *Guernica*, *Horsethief*, *H.O.W. Journal*, *The Iowa Review*, *The Journal*, *Kenyon Review Online*, *La Presa*, *The Los Angeles Review*, *Narrative Magazine*, *The New Yorker*, *Parnassus*, *Plume*, *Storyscape*, *Tupelo Quarterly*, *Two Peach*, *The Yale Review*.

Thank you to the judges of the 2016 Juniper Prize, Dara Wier and James Haug, and to Karen Fisk, Carol Betsch, and Sally Nichols, the wizards of University of Massachusetts Press, for making book publishing seem like a magic trick. Thank you to the many friends, relatives, writers, colleagues, strangers, and teachers who have welcomed, fed, and grown me as a poet. First, thank you to my mother for all the notebooks, all the listening, all the anxiety, and all the love. Thank you to Estelle Shane who helped me be strong enough to revise my self with my poems. Thank you, Debbie Attanasio, for knowing all the rules and catching my grammatical delinquents.

For their timeless and infinite guidance word-wise and heart-wise, thank you to my mentors and readers: Christine Schutt for calling me a writer first and for the first brutal scissors; Julie Whitaker for keeping everything no matter what and for modeling the artful life; Jean Valentine for your talismanic salvations; Alice Quinn for your devoted stewardship; Josh Bell for teaching me about devotion; Lee Briccetti for teaching me the importance of a poetry home and community; Danny Loedel for being my first writing partner in crime, co-conspirator, critic, dreamer, skeptic, and believer; Michael Weinstein for being one awesome step ahead and inspiring my belief in the poetry of ideas; Richard Howard for bestowing the whole tradition to me as if it were a secret; Frank Bidart for teaching me that voice is the best measure of clarity.

Thank you, Columbia University, for the time, funding, and family: Thank you, Dorothea Lasky, for your witchy brilliance, your never saying No, your secret keys to poems, your love affairs with the future, and for including me in the possibilities. Thank you, Timothy Donnelly, for bringing out the wildest me, for teaching me that poems can think as well as people. Thank you for your bottomless brain, psychic heart, and extraterrestrial genius. To my undreamable Sister and spiritual guide, Lucie Brock-Broido, thank you for the first spirit paper—and then of course all the others. Thank you for saving my life, always twice: then and now, *if I needed you.*

Thank you to Max Ritvo, whose daemon I am most indebted to, and for whom most of this book was written. Max, you have taught me that the heart has infinite hooks and can hold anything and be held by anything. You have taught me that the universe is a matter of multiplying one soul by the unknown. You've taught me that poetry is the best way to love time and that language is just like eye contact but between thoughts and that a self is just a hilarious tableau vivant for thinking. You've taught me that writing is a way to worship, commune, and entertain. Thank you for reincarnating me into a wider, wilder, funnier, more rational, more imaginative, more loving, more ethical person and poet. Let's hold mirrors over each other's words wherever we are so we can read each other read. You cannot go missing in me.

Above all, to my life partner, Dan Attanasio—who needs no words and knows all the words—for being my first empathic reader and my last ruthless editor, thank you for staying up with me, for holding me up, for writing and rewriting each poem with me with your love and

Acknowledgments

your candor, and for understanding what I mean before I say it and sometimes before I mean it. You have shown me that the I is the You and the You is the I and that meaning is what not knowing teaches us. These poems are for you, with you, and by you. Authorship is just the name of our spaceship. For seven years, you have turned every doubt and dry-spell into the wonder from which I write. I once asked you if you would love me if I stopped being a poet and you said No. Thank you.

JUNIPER
JUNIPER PRIZE FOR POETRY

This volume is the forty-first recipient of the
Juniper Prize for Poetry, established in 1975 by the
University of Massachusetts Press in collaboration with
the UMass Amherst MFA program for Poets and Writers.
The prize is named in honor of the poet Robert Francis
(1901–1987), who for many years lived in Fort Juniper,
a tiny home of his own construction, in Amherst.